*Every new generation of children is enthralled by the famous stories in our Well Loved Tales series. Younger ones love to have the story read to them. Older children will enjoy the exciting stories in an easy-to-read text.*

Published by Ladybird Books Ltd  Loughborough  Leicestershire  UK
Ladybird Books Inc  Auburn  Maine 04210  USA

WELL LOVED TALES

# Snow White
# and the
# Seven Dwarfs

retold for easy reading
by VERA SOUTHGATE M A B Com
with illustrations by MARTIN AITCHISON

Ladybird Books

Once upon a time, on a cold winter's day, as
the snowflakes were falling softly and swiftly, a
Queen sat sewing by her window. As she looked
out, the snow scene was framed, like a picture,
by the black ebony of the window frame.

As she sewed, the Queen pricked her finger and three drops of blood fell upon her sewing. The red of the blood, against the white of the snow, framed by the black wood of the window frame, looked so beautiful that she thought, "O how I wish I could have a child as white as snow, as red as blood and as black as ebony!"

Now it happened that some time afterwards the Queen did have a baby daughter whose skin was as white as snow, whose cheeks were bright red and whose hair was as black as ebony. The Queen called her little girl Snow White.

Unfortunately, soon after her child was born, the Queen died. A year later the King married again.

The new Queen was very beautiful but much too proud of her own beauty. She could not bear to think that anyone else might be more beautiful.

The Queen had a magic looking-glass which hung on the wall. Often she stood in front of it and, gazing at her own reflection, asked this question,

"Mirror, mirror, on the wall,

Among the ladies in this land,

Who is the fairest of them all?"

The mirror always replied,

"Thou, O Queen, art the fairest of all!"

The Queen was always content when she heard this reply for she knew that the magic mirror could speak nothing but the truth.

Meanwhile, Snow White was growing from a baby into a lovely little girl. By the time she was seven, with her rosy cheeks and dark, dark hair against her snow white skin, she was even more beautiful than the Queen.

Thus it happened that one day, when the Queen asked her mirror,

"Mirror, mirror, on the wall,

Among the ladies in this land,

Who is the fairest of them all?"

it replied,

"Among the grown-up ladies tall,
   Thou, O Queen, art the fairest of all.
   Yet the truth I must speak
      and so I do vow,
   That the child Snow White is more
      lovely than thou."

When the Queen heard these words, she was both shocked and angry. She looked more closely at Snow White and could not fail to see her growing beauty. Each day, as she watched the girl, the Queen's anger and jealousy increased.

At length, the time came when the Queen's envy of Snow White's beauty gave her no peace, by day or by night. Hatred for the child filled her heart. Then the Queen called one of her huntsmen and commanded him, "Take this child away, deep into the forest and kill her, for I can no longer bear the sight of her!"

The huntsman had no choice but to obey. Taking Snow White by the hand, he led her far into the forest. When he stopped and drew out his knife to kill her, the poor child wept and begged him to spare her life. "Please do not kill me," she pleaded. "If you will spare me, I shall go further into the forest and I promise never to try to return home again."

When the huntsman saw the tears on such a young and beautiful face, he took pity on her. "Run away then, my poor child," he said, as he put away his knife. "The wild beasts will soon devour the poor child," he thought to himself.

When Snow White ran off into the great forest by herself, she was terrified. She did not know which way to go, nor yet what would happen to her. She feared she would meet wild beasts which would attack her.

She ran on and on, over sharp stones and round prickly bushes with long thorns. She heard the roars of wild beasts but, although some

passed her as she ran, none tried to harm her. By evening her feet were sore, her clothes were torn and her arms and legs were scratched by the thorns.

Just as Snow White was ready to fall down with weariness, she came to a little cottage, by the side of a mountain. She knocked on the door but there was no reply. She tried the door and it opened, so she went inside to rest.

Everything inside the cottage was small and neat and clean. A white cloth was spread on the table. The table was laid with seven little plates, seven little knives, forks and spoons, and seven little glasses, all set out in proper order. Against the wall stood seven little beds, each neatly made up and covered with a white bedspread.

GOD BLESS

Snow White was both hungry and thirsty but she did not want to take anyone's supper. So she ate a little of the food from each plate and drank a mouthful of wine from each glass.

Then Snow White was so tired that she longed to sleep. She lay down on the first little bed but somehow she could not make herself comfortable. She tried the other little beds but each one seemed too long or too short, too hard or too soft. None suited her until she came to the last one, which felt just right. Soon she was fast asleep.

Now the cottage belonged to seven dwarfs who, when it became dark, returned home. They had spent all day in the mountains, digging for gold.

As they entered their cottage, each one lit a candle. By the light of the seven candles, they could see that someone had been there since they had left that morning.

The first dwarf cried, "Who has been sitting on my chair?"

The second one asked, "Who has been eating from my plate?"

The third one asked, "Who has been eating my bread?"

The fourth one asked, "Who has been eating my vegetables?"

The fifth one asked, "Who has been using my knife?"

The sixth one asked, "Who has been using my fork?"

The seventh one asked, "Who has been drinking out of my glass?"

Next the dwarfs noticed that their beds were not as neat as when they had left them. The first dwarf looked at his bed and cried, "Who has been lying in my bed?"

Then each of the other dwarfs, in turn, looked at his own bed and cried, "Who has been lying in my bed?"

But when the seventh little dwarf reached his bed, he found Snow White there, fast asleep. "Look who's in my bed!" he called to the others and they all came running to see.

They lifted their candlesticks high, as they stood around the bed, gazing at Snow White. "What a beautiful child!" they exclaimed.

As the dwarfs were anxious not to waken the lovely child who slept so soundly, they tiptoed away and ate their suppers very quietly. Then when bedtime came, the seventh little dwarf spent an hour in the bed of each of the other dwarfs, in turn, and so the night passed.

In the morning, when Snow White first awoke and saw the seven dwarfs, she was rather frightened. The dwarfs however spoke kindly to her and asked her name. "My name is Snow White," she replied.

"But how did you find our cottage?" they asked.

Snow White told them about her stepmother who had sent a huntsman with her into the forest, to kill her, and how the huntsman had agreed to spare her life. "Then I ran and ran all day through the forest," she continued, "until I came to this little cottage." When the dwarfs heard this sad tale they were full of pity for the little girl. The eldest one told her, "If you will look after us, keep our house clean and tidy, cook and wash and mend for us, you can live here with us and we shall take good care of you."

"Oh, you are kind!" replied Snow White. "I shall be glad to do that."

However, before they left the house, the dwarfs gave Snow White a warning. "We are out all day, working," they said, "and you will be alone in the house. If your stepmother learns that you are here, she may come and try to do you harm. So be sure to let no one into the house while we are away." Snow White promised to heed their warning.

She was very happy living with the dwarfs. Every morning they went off to the mountains to dig for gold. Every evening when they returned home, she had supper ready for them and the house was neat and clean. Although Snow White was alone all day, she did not feel lonely for she had so many things to do.

Meanwhile the Queen, believing Snow White to be dead, was quite happy in the thought that she herself was the most beautiful lady in the land. It was some time before she bothered to ask the magic mirror the usual question.

When she did stand before the mirror and said,
"Mirror, mirror, on the wall,
Among the ladies in this land,
Who is the fairest of them all?"
she could not believe her ears when she heard this reply,
"Thou, O Queen, art exceedingly fair,
But the truth I must speak
and this I do swear,
Snow White is not dead but living still,
In a little house far over the hill;
And though thou, O Queen,
art certainly fair,
This child's great beauty doth
make her more fair."

Then great was the anger of the Queen. She knew that as the mirror never lied, her huntsman must have deceived her.

The Queen's jealousy would not let her rest as long as she knew that anyone was more beautiful than she was. She determined to find Snow White and kill her herself.

But how could she do this? She knew that she must not let Snow White recognise her. Finally, she decided to disguise herself as an old pedlar-woman who called at people's houses, selling things from her basket. She dressed herself in old clothes and changed her face. No one could possibly have recognised the beautiful Queen.

She then travelled through the forest until she came to the dwarfs' cottage by the mountain. She knocked on the door and shouted, "Laces and ribbons for sale! Pretty laces and ribbons!"

Snow White looked out of the window and thought to herself, "What harm can this poor old woman do to me?"

Snow White opened the door and the woman brought her basket into the cottage. Snow White chose some pretty pink laces for her stays.

The old woman offered to lace up Snow White's corset, properly, with the new laces. Snow White, suspecting nothing, agreed. Then the Queen laced her so tightly that the child could not breathe, and she fell on the floor as if she were dead.

In the evening, when the dwarfs returned home, they were shocked to find their beloved Snow White lying on the floor as if she were dead. They lifted her up tenderly and, when they saw how tightly she was laced, they cut the new laces. Soon she began to breathe again and gradually the colour returned to her cheeks.

When the dwarfs heard about the pedlar-woman, they were convinced that she must have been Snow White's wicked stepmother.

The dwarfs warned Snow White again, "Take great care and be sure to let no one enter the house."

The Queen hurried back through the forest. She was filled with joy because, believing Snow White to be dead, she herself must now be fairest of all.

As soon as she reached home, she removed her disguise and stood before her mirror, asking,

"Mirror, mirror, on the wall,
    Among the ladies in this land,
    Who is the fairest of them all?"

You can imagine the rage into which she flew when the mirror replied,

"Thou, O Queen, art exceedingly fair,
    But the truth I must speak
        and this I do swear,
    Snow White is not dead but living still,
    In a little house far over the hill;
    And though thou, O Queen,
        art certainly fair,
    This child's great beauty doth
        make her more fair."

So, once more the Queen began to plan how she might kill Snow White. First, she prepared a comb which was poisoned. Next, she disguised herself as a quite different pedlar-woman and filled her basket with new things to sell.

Again she travelled through the forest until she came to the dwarfs' cottage by the side of the mountain. She knocked on the door and shouted, "Cheap wares to sell! Pretty things to sell!"

Snow White put her head out of the window. "I dare not let you come in," she said, "I have promised the dwarfs to open the door to no one."

"Never mind! You can look, can't you?"
replied the Queen, holding up the dainty comb.
It was so pretty that Snow White could not resist
it and she opened the door to the pedlar-woman.

The old woman said, "You must let me comb your hair properly for you." Snow White agreed and seated herself on a stool. The Queen then stuck the comb sharply into Snow White's head so that the poison went into her blood. Immediately she fell to the floor, as if dead.

Fortunately, it was almost evening and soon afterwards the seven dwarfs came home. When they found Snow White once more lying on the floor, they suspected that her stepmother had been again. They soon found the poisoned comb and pulled it out. Snow White quickly recovered and told them what had happened.

Once more the dwarfs talked seriously to her. They warned her of the wickedness of her stepmother and begged her never to let anyone enter the house while they were out.

Meanwhile the Queen
was hurrying through the forest,
muttering to herself, "I've killed her
this time! I've killed her this time!"

On reaching home, she removed her disguise
and stood before the mirror, asking,

"Mirror, mirror, on the wall,
Among the ladies in this land,
Who is the fairest of them all?"

Just as before the mirror replied,

"Thou, O Queen, art exceedingly fair,
But the truth I must speak
and this I do swear,
Snow White is not dead but living still,
In a little house far over the hill;
And though thou, O Queen,
art certainly fair,
This child's great beauty doth
make her more fair."

At these words, the Queen stamped her feet and beat on the looking-glass in her rage. "Snow White shall die," she vowed, "even if it costs me my life!"

The Queen knew that it might prove impossible to persuade Snow White to let her into the cottage a third time, so she plotted cunningly.

She took a lovely apple which had one green cheek and one rosy cheek. It looked so tempting that anyone who saw it must long to eat it. Then she put poison into the red cheek of the apple,

while leaving the green side free of poison.

This time, the Queen filled her basket with apples and disguised herself as a farmer's wife. For the third time, she made her way to the dwarfs' cottage and knocked on the door.

"I am forbidden to open the door to anyone," called Snow White through the window.

"It's all the same to me!" replied the farmer's wife. "I only want to get rid of these apples. Here, I'll give this one to you," she went on, holding out the poisoned apple to Snow White.

"I dare not take it," replied Snow White, shaking her head.

The farmer's wife laughed pleasantly. "Are you afraid that it's poisoned?" she joked. "Look, I'll cut it in two and we shall each eat half." This she did, holding out the rosy half of the apple to Snow White and biting into the green half herself.

Snow White longed to eat the rosy half of the apple, which looked so tempting. When she saw the woman happily eating one half of the apple, she thought there could be no harm in eating the other half herself. So she took the rosy half of the apple and bit into it. No sooner had she done so than she fell down dead.

The Queen laughed a horrible laugh and cried, "This time the dwarfs won't waken you!"

Then the Queen returned to her palace and asked her mirror,

"Mirror, mirror, on the wall,
Among the ladies in this land,
Who is the fairest of them all?"

At long last it answered,

"Thou, O Queen, art the fairest of all!"
Thus the jealous Queen was finally content.

When the dwarfs returned home in the

evening, there lay Snow White on the floor, no longer breathing. Yet they still hoped that they might be able to revive her. They unlaced her stays, combed her hair and washed her face, but they could not find how she had died.

The dwarfs were heart-broken. They stood round her and wept, saying, "Our beautiful Snow White is dead!" For three days and nights they stood round her, mourning.

At the end of three days, the dwarfs knew they must bury their beloved Snow White. Yet they could not bear to do so, for she looked as though she were still alive.

So they had a glass coffin made, in order that they might still see her. They wrote on the side, in

letters of gold, that her name was Snow White
and that she was a king's daughter. The dwarfs
carried the glass coffin to the top of the
mountain. Then they each took it in turn to sit
always by the coffin, day and night.

There Snow White lay, as if still alive, but
sleeping, with her skin as white as snow, her
cheeks as red as blood and her hair as black as
ebony. Even the birds came and wept to see her
lying so still.

Snow White lay in the glass coffin for many years and still she looked as if she were alive and only sleeping.

One day, it happened that a king's son found the glass coffin on the top of the mountain. He could not take his eyes from the beautiful girl within it. He gazed at her and fell in love with her.

"Let me have the coffin," he begged the dwarfs, "and I will give you whatever you ask."

But they only answered, "We would not part with Snow White for all the gold in the world."

The Prince continued to plead with them. "I cannot live without her," he said. "If you will give her to me, I shall cherish her all my life."

At length the dwarfs took pity on the Prince and agreed to give him the coffin.

As the Prince's servants were carrying the coffin down the mountainside, they stumbled on the roots of a tree. The coffin was so badly jolted that the piece of apple, which had stuck in Snow White's throat, was flung out. She opened her eyes, lifted up the lid of the coffin and sat up. "Where am I?" she cried, in surprise.

The Prince was overjoyed to see her alive. He told her all that had happened and how he had fallen in love with her. "Come with me to my father's palace and we shall be married," he begged, and Snow White agreed.

She said goodbye to the dwarfs who had been so kind to her and had loved her so dearly. Although they were sad to lose her, they were content to know that she was alive and that she would be happy with the Prince.

A magnificent wedding feast was arranged for Snow White and the Prince. And it happened that Snow White's stepmother was among those invited to the feast. When the Queen, dressed in her finest clothes, was ready for the wedding, she stood before her mirror and asked,

"Mirror, mirror, on the wall,

Among the ladies in this land,

Who is the fairest of them all?"

The mirror replied,

"Thou, O Queen, art exceedingly fair,

But the truth I must speak

and so I do vow,

That the young bride-to-be is more

lovely than thou!"

These words so angered the Queen that, at first, she felt she could not bear to go to the

wedding. Later, she felt she must see this new young Queen. Of course, when she arrived at the feast, she recognised Snow White! Her rage was so great that she fell down and had to be taken home, where soon afterwards she died.